A Richard Jackson Book

"Never Spit on Your Shoes"

by DENYS CAZET

ORCHARD BOOKS · NEW YORK

Also by the author

Mother Night
Great-uncle Felix
A Fish in His Pocket

Orchard Books, A division of Franklin Watts, Inc.
387 Park Avenue South, New York, NY 10016

Manufactured in the United States of America. Printed by General Offset Co., Inc. Bound by
Horowitz/Rae. Book design by Mina Greenstein.
The text of this book is set in 16 pt. ITC Bookman Light. The illustrations are watercolor
paintings, reproduced in halftone.

10 9 8 7 6 5 4 3 2 1

Library of Congress Cataloging-in-Publication Data
Cazet, Denys. Never spit on your shoes / by Denys Cazet. p.   cm. "A Richard Jackson
book." Summary: First grader Arnie tells his mother about his tiring first day at
school, while the illustrations reveal the mayhem he is leaving out of his account.
ISBN 0-531-05847-6. ISBN 0-531-08447-7 (lib. bdg.) [1.Schools—Fiction.]
I. Title. PZ7.C2985Ne 1990 [E]—dc20 89-35164 CIP AC

for my little sister, Andree,
and of course, Don, Michael, and Amy

Arnie slammed the screen door and flopped
into a chair.

"Milk!" he gasped.

Arnie's mother poured cold milk into a glass.

"Well?" she said. "How was Mr. First Grader's first day?"

"You have to find a desk with your name on it," Arnie said. "It's hard work."

"Finding your desk?"

"Sitting in it," said Arnie.

Mother put some cookies on the table.

"We had to sit together in a circle and help the teacher make the rules."

Is it time to go home?

Arnie picked up a cookie.
"Never spit on your shoes," he said.
"I promise," said Mother.

"We went on a tour," Arnie continued. "The teacher showed us where the principal lives. She showed us the playground and the bathrooms."

"At recess I learned how to spell *boys*," Arnie said. "B-o-y-s."

"Perfect," said Mother.

Arnie picked up another cookie. "Don't you want one?"

"Just one," she said. "I'm on a new diet."

"We used our new crayons," Arnie went on. "Remember when Uncle Willie jumped into the pool and his swimsuit came off?"

Mother's eyebrows popped up. "*That's* what you drew?"

"I didn't finish," Arnie said. "My yellow skidded and hit Raymond."

...new shoes.

Arnie's mother reached for another cookie.
"Is your diet over?"
Mother put the cookie back.
"Who is Raymond?" she asked.

"He's new," Arnie said. "Raymond can write
his name backwards."

. . . ick!

"We ate our lunch together in the cafeteria."

Arnie slumped across the kitchen table.
"Do you want to take a nap?" Mother asked.

Arnie sat up. "No naps in the first grade," he said. "After lunch, the teacher told us a story, and some kids cried."

"My goodness. It must have been a very sad story."

Arnie sighed. "We saw our old kindergarten bus going home."

Arnie's mother brushed his hair.

"Did you have to do any arithmetic?" she asked.

"Math," Arnie corrected. "Right after recess."

"I helped Raymond count to sixteen."

"In P.E., I was a prisoner," said Arnie.
"Raymond tagged me free."
"Thank goodness for Raymond," said Mother.

Arnie ate another cookie. "After P.E., the teacher read us a story about a giant." "Was it scary?"

Arnie shrugged. "I fell asleep."

"And now," said Mother, "here you are."

Arnie slid off the chair. He reached into his backpack and pulled out a piece of paper.

"Field trip," he said. "You have to sign this."

"A field trip, already?"

"Yep," said Arnie. "We're going to the aquarium."

He picked up his backpack. "I have to get ready."
"Arnie, you're not going until next Friday!"
"I know," he answered. "But I don't remember
where I put my swim fins."

Arnie's mother ate another cookie.